A.R. BLASTS OFF!

Charles Hirsch
Illustrated by Melisande Potter

Rigby

CONTENTS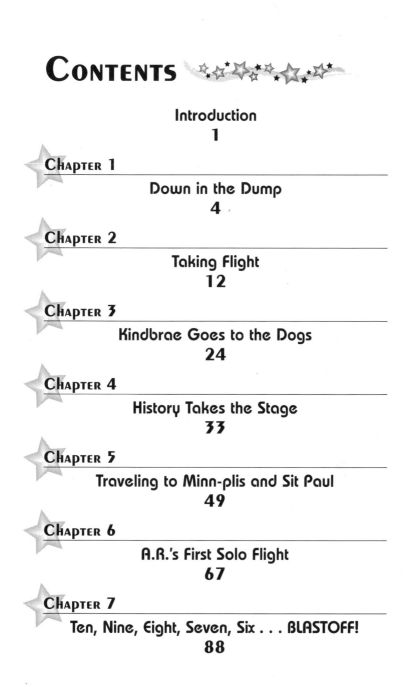

Introduction
1

CHAPTER 1

Down in the Dump
4

CHAPTER 2

Taking Flight
12

CHAPTER 3

Kindbrae Goes to the Dogs
24

CHAPTER 4

History Takes the Stage
33

CHAPTER 5

Traveling to Minn-plis and Sit Paul
49

CHAPTER 6

A.R.'s First Solo Flight
67

CHAPTER 7

Ten, Nine, Eight, Seven, Six . . . BLASTOFF!
88

Introduction

Kindbrae, Minnesota (population 49), is located at the southwest corner of Minnesota, where it practically reaches out and shakes hands with its neighboring states, South Dakota and Iowa. Here the Great Plains roll out like a carpet on their way to meet the Rocky Mountains. The big Twin Cities of Minneapolis and St. Paul, which the Kindbrae folks call the Cities, are about 125 miles away.

That summer, not a lot happened in Kindbrae that you might read about in the history books. The sun rose. The sun set. Each day had 24 hours. The six potted trees that lined Main Street continued to inch their way up toward the sun. Down at the edge of town, the mighty Little Mudslinger River still ran downstream. It didn't hop, skip, or jump. No volcanoes erupted. No avalanches occurred. There were two tornado warnings that got everyone excited, but they turned out to be only severe thunderstorms. The President of the United States didn't come to visit. No president ever did visit Kindbrae, Minnesota.

A few notable things did happen, though. Roberta and Bob Bobbe's horse, Shawn, gave birth to a pretty new foal that they named "Bathtub." She was all white with a black ring around her belly. In that same week, Kindbrae hit an almost record-high June temperature of 110 degrees for three days in a row. According to Lloyd Meisterteister (pronounced my-stir-ty-stir), the record was set in the summer of 1957. People remember Lloyd frying an egg on the hood of his pickup truck right in front of the Kindbrae General Store and Cafe, which he and his wife, Flo, have run all these years.

Customers would greet Flo and Lloyd at the cafe with, "Hot enough for you?"

"No," Lloyd would say, "I think I'll turn on the heater and stoke up the oven."

At the Kindbrae General Store and Cafe (the cafe part), they kept on cooking no matter how hot it got. People expected the cafe to stick to its weekly menu. It was always hamburgers on Tuesdays, Fridays, and Saturdays, and frog legs and french fries on Mondays Wednesdays, and Thursdays. The cafe was closed on Sundays. They kept on cooking even if it was 110 degrees in the shade or 30 degrees below zero.

The Kindbrae General Store and Cafe was Kindbrae's heart. Lloyd and Flo Meisterteister provided the people in Kindbrae with just about all the things that they needed. Lloyd carried 25 kinds of canned goods, a dozen or so things in jars, several brands of soda pop, and a variety of stationery, pens, and pencils. In other words, things that people "generally" needed. And Lloyd would order or go get anything anyone wanted if they gave him a few days' notice.

But more importantly, Lloyd kept track of everyone's comings and goings. Like his father before him, Lloyd was the Official Town Historian. If you spent a day at the General Store and Cafe you'd meet just about everyone in town. Lloyd would talk your ear off.

Most days you'd find nine-year-old Aida Rose Smith at the cafe. She listened and learned from Lloyd. But sometimes his stories got too shaggy, like a bad haircut. Aida Rose would clap her hands over her ears and yell, "You're OFF the subject!" And in response, Lloyd would put his story right back on track, as if it were a toy railroad car.

Aida Rose didn't know it, but by summer's end she would become one of the most important figures in the history of Kindbrae, MN. This was the summer Aida Rose blasted off.

And this is the story of her achievement.

CHAPTER 1

Down in the Dump

The first day of summer vacation began just like the summer before. Aida Rose Smith was at work in the garden. The summer before that, when she was seven years old, work in the garden was almost all play and no work. She would use the rake as a horse and ride around like a knight protecting her castle from enemy attack. When she was seven, she could go to the reading hour at the Bookmobile and play whenever she wanted to with Becky Lambordini, her best friend.

Aida Rose and Becky would go off to their secret hiding place in the pine grove behind the Kindbrae Town Dump and Recycling Center. Tiny Sybrandt and Big Glenn, who ran the center, took recycling very seriously. Tiny Sybrandt was six-foot-two and weighed 280 pounds. Big Glenn was five-foot-three and weighed 102 pounds on the button. Tiny and Glenn thought they helped keep the *kind* in

Kindbrae. They expected people to be kind to one another and also made sure that people thought kindly of their possessions.

At the Kindbrae Town Dump and Recycling Center, there was a place for everything and everything had its place: newspapers, cans, blue bottles, green bottles, brown bottles, clear bottles—all were neatly sorted. Of course, the smelly and totally unusable garbage and trash went into the dumpster. However, the Kindbrae Town Dump and Recycling Center Committee made sure that its good citizens didn't throw away anything that could be used again. Both Tiny and Big Glenn kept an eagle eye on everything that came and went. They were no-nonsense types when it came to what anyone could throw away.

"Why are you throwing out that perfectly good sofa?" Big Glenn once asked Trixie O'Rourke. "You go home and wear that out before you throw it away."

So now Trixie has both a new and an old sofa in her living room. Trixie's guests are only allowed to sit on the old sofa. She hopes they'll wear it out so Tiny and Big Glenn will let her get rid of it.

Still-usable things were placed outside the dump's fence under a sign that read, "Still Good After All These Years." Tiny and Big Glenn believed that one person's throwaway, with a little imagination and some elbow grease, could become another person's treasure.

Tiny Sybrandt made most of the creative decisions. He cut buttons off old clothes, sorted them by color and size, and made them into mosaic pictures that he displayed at the County Fair. "Old bathtubs make good watering troughs," he pointed out. "Patch those old tractor tire inner tubes. They make for fine floating on a lazy afternoon in Drie Lake." As a matter of fact, the chairs in the Kindbrae General Store and Cafe came from the dump. Tiny and Big Glenn didn't see their jobs as disposing of waste, but trying to prevent it in the first place.

Sometimes Aida Rose and Becky would borrow things from the recycling center. In their secret play area, Aida Rose and Becky built a clubhouse from a discarded refrigerator box and an abandoned bookcase. They were like architects, using whatever they could drag from the things piled under the sign, "Still Good After All These Years." One day they built a fort. Another day they constructed a barn. One time Aida Rose brought her pet chicken, Peeper, along. So Becky went home to get Dewey, the family cat. The animals didn't get along too well, so the girls decided that from then on they shouldn't care for any livestock. Instead, they'd dig up little clumps of dandelions and arrange them in rows around the barn as though they were fields of corn. They decided that they'd just raise animal feed and when they made enough money, they'd buy a pony. A real pony!

Most of the time they invented their own games. They would take the tomato sauce cans recycled from the school lunch program and jump on the cans and scrunch the center so their feet could be wedged in. They'd walk around in their tin-can shoes, challenging each other.

"I'm bigger than you!" Aida Rose would say as she hobbled around.

"I'm bigger than you!" Becky would say back as she lifted herself up a full inch and a half taller than Aida Rose.

Sometimes they'd bring out peanut butter and strawberry jelly sandwiches, along with pillows and blankets from home. They'd picnic in their playhouse. They talked about times when they might have sleepovers. In their cozy home, Aida Rose and Becky would dream dreams.

"I'm going to be a doctor," Becky would say. "And I'm going to go to Norway or Canada and cure diseases." Becky had seen a television program about Norway and decided it would be a good place to help people. As for Canada, she had always wanted to go there to meet a member of the Royal Canadian Mounted Police, like the ones she saw on TV.

"Not me," Aida Rose said. "I'm going to be Superwoman and fly around the world. Maybe I'll fly over to Norway. We'll be best friends even when we're old and wear lipstick.

"Or maybe I'll be an astronaut," she continued, "and I'll fly through space." Already at age seven, Aida Rose had her sights set skyward.

One time she convinced Becky to help her make a space station. They dragged two old tires into their play area. On top of the tires they placed a cardboard box big enough to sit in. They wedged a broomstick upright in one corner of the box and balanced a bicycle wheel on top of the broomstick. A broken boombox was set up as a control panel.

The next day, Aida Rose snuck out of the house with Big Brother Billy's model space vehicles. She borrowed his Skyrocket III, his prized electronic Moonrover, and his Super Stealth IV. Aida Rose even brought along the Skyrocket launcher, but she forgot the batteries. The girls built three dirt piles around their space station. They placed each of Big Brother Billy's models on one of the dirt piles, ready for take off. The space station would launch them all into the solar system. They would travel to the stars.

Aida Rose climbed inside the box. Then she started moving back and forth and bounced up and down.

"Ten, nine, eight, seven, six. Blast off!" she yelled.

With that, Becky followed Aida Rose's instructions to push. Aida Rose and the box tumbled forward. *Crunch!* The sound of a crushed Moonrover ended their space flight.

"Oh no!" were the last words heard coming from the space station.

"Aida Rose, how, how, *how* could you . . ." Big Brother Billy's voice trailed off when his little sister showed him the grocery bag holding his muddy Skyrocket III and Super Stealth IV, along with what was left of the Moonrover.

What followed was Aida Rose's first lesson in what her father called *responsibility*. Aida Rose had $12.38 in her clown bank. It was saved from the birthday money that her grandmother had sent. Aida Rose's parents, after a long discussion, decided that $11.00 of it should go to Big Brother Billy.

News of the broken Moonrover reached Becky's parents, and Becky came by the next day with an additional $5.00 contribution. Becky was instructed not even to think about keeping the money for herself, although Becky thought it was fun to think about what she and Aida Rose could buy with $5.00 at the General Store.

That night Aida Rose had a dream. She floated down the Little Mudslinger River. As she rounded the bend, she saw a group of aliens. She went on shore and the aliens handed her keys to a life-size Moonrover, which they told her was parked in her secret play area. She returned home and presented the keys to Big Brother Billy, which made him very happy. Aida Rose liked space dreams.

That was two summers ago.

Chapter 2

Taking Flight

This was the summer that Aida Rose and her brother became partners and co-owners of the Smith Family's Garden and Farm Stand.

The Smith's garden was more than a border of flowers growing around the house. When Aida Rose wanted to impress visitors, she would explain that the garden was almost three acres—at least the size of a city block. Sometimes Aida Rose imagined it was the Smith Family's Secret Garden, a garden with a tall stone wall where she could hide away and play with mysterious friends and wild beasts. But in reality, it would be hard to keep two-and-a-half acres a secret.

In this part of the United States, the Midwest, this type of garden is known as a "truck garden." Aida Rose would explain, "A truck garden grows all kinds of flowers and vegetables. We grow lettuce, beets, carrots, peas, beans, and corn, and we truck them to market." She'd go on with her list, finally ending by telling you, "We call it a truck garden because with all the work we have to do, we have to keep on trucking."

She made it sound as if she had to go it alone. But she had help, of course. Big Brother Billy helped. Her father did the tilling, turning the soil so it was soft and ready for planting. Mom did the mulching, spreading hay around the plants. It helped them keep cool, she explained.

This garden, as Mr. and Mrs. Smith often reminded their children, was both Aida Rose's and her brother's responsibility. *Responsibility.* Big Brother Billy understood responsibility. It meant you did four hours of work and then you went and did two hours of stuff with your friends. It meant that you had to watch the farm stand. Billy acted responsibly—in other words—like a big brother. To Aida, "Big Brother Billy" was practically the only name she ever heard since she was born. Big Brother Billy will watch you. Big Brother Billy will take you to school. Big Brother Billy will play with you.

So, if Billy was "Big Brother Billy," did that make Aida Rose "Little Sister Aida Rose"? No way! It was bad enough that she had two names—Aida and Rose. She never wanted to be known to the world as Little Sister Aida Rose. That was worse than having Becky's nickname—*Snuckergans*—a word that meant "chatty goose" to the people of Kindbrae.

Ever since Becky was a baby, she would coo and

chat. When Flo Meisterteister first laid eyes on Becky, who was cooing and chatting and being ever so cute, she said, "What a little *snuckergans.*" The nickname stuck. Becky stayed cute and she also kept on being chatty.

Becky moved away from Kindbrae when she was seven, but everyone thought she probably kept on being chatty. Soon Lily Sue Jeffrey moved into Becky's house and took on the title of "New Best Friend" to Aida Rose.

Aida Rose's thoughts went back to the subject of responsibility. *Responsibility.* How Aida Rose cringed when she heard that word. It meant planting and weeding and picking. It did *not* mean going swimming or watching the Exploration Channel on TV—Aida Rose's favorite of all the gazillion stations they could get on their digital satellite dish.

Mr. Smith, whom Aida Rose called "Pappy," also referred to his kids' garden as their "bank account" because the money they earned from it went into a special bank account that they would use for their college education or, if necessary, for an emergency. Aida Rose thought an emergency had to be something so tremendously gigantic that it was almost too scary to imagine.

So instead, Aida Rose liked to think that a

tremendously gigantic emergency might mean a family vacation to Mars. Aida Rose dreamed and planned for the day when space travel was so commonplace that people flew off to the solar system just like people visited the Grand Canyon or Mount Rushmore. Her family might not take a Mars vacation this summer, but soon, Aida Rose hoped. When Martian vacations were possible, Aida Rose wanted her family to be the first to go. Now *that* would be worth working for.

Mr. Smith also referred to their garden as "pay dirt." He meant that the dirt in the garden was just like cash. Plants grew out of the dirt and produced vegetables. The vegetables were sold. The money they made from selling the vegetables paid for the things the Smiths bought, hence the term "pay dirt."

"In this rich soil grow the seeds of learning," Mr. Smith would say in his deep voice, almost singing it like an opera singer.

Aida Rose would rap to herself:

"Plant the seeds. There ain't nothing to it.
Let's go to Mars.
We gotta, gotta do it."

Other times Pappy would say, "In this rich soil grows the down payment on our new car . . ." or "In this rich soil sprouts a new computer with a faster modem and lots more megabytes of memory." (Aida Rose liked that idea of pay dirt.)

Pappy had plenty to sing about. Aida Rose and Big Brother Billy's garden was only one-tenth of a percent of the total farm. Their whole farm was over 2,000 acres. The other 99.9 percent of the farm grew soybeans, corn, and wheat. Bushels of these crops left the farm for places all over the world to be ground into grain for cereal and feed for cattle.

Pappy, whose singing (to most people) sounded like a CD does when it skips, would have been flattered to think that Aida Rose compared him to an opera singer. He really was quite an opera fan. When he was working the fields, he would listen to CDs of operas in the cab of his tractor. He loved opera so much that he named his daughter Aida Rose after his favorite opera, *Aida*. It's about the princess daughter of an Ethiopian king who was kidnapped and brought to Egypt. Her parents chose the second name, *Rose,* because it was her mother's favorite flower and her mom thought it was a beautiful name. Sometimes when she would call out her daughter's name, she would think of special occasions when Pappy sent roses, like her birthday or their wedding anniversary.

"Oh, Aida Rose," Mom would start to say, "I remember when your father brought me roses." And

Aida Rose knew she was in for what she thought was some dumb, mushy story. Her mom might tell her about the time when Pappy sent her a dozen roses on their first Valentine's Day together. Or she might tell about the time Pappy surprised her with roses the day after they moved into their new house and found out the roof leaked.

At age eight-and-a-half, Aida Rose decided that she didn't want to listen to any more romantic stories just because of her name. "I'm changing my name," she announced at breakfast one morning.

"Starting today, I'm going to be called A.R. Smith." It was a name that sounded so grown-up to Aida Rose. It was a name like a famous author's or somebody who was at least thirty years old. It was a name that sounded just right to the ears of Aida Rose Smith. So from then on she was A.R., and when people forgot and called her Aida Rose, she corrected them.

On the first day of summer vacation of the first year of the millennium, A.R. was smack in the middle of the new lettuces, going row by row, cutting one head after another. For the occasion, she was dressed all in green. She wore green tights, her aquamarine bathing suit, and a green felt cape. She had a three-cornered hat made from green construction paper with a long goose feather sticking out.

"Pick one, hurl two, pick and weed is all we do," she chanted as she hurled one head of lettuce after another into a crate. Snip. Toss. Snip. Toss. A.R. Smith looked like a four-foot-eight green machine.

"One crate down, nine to go. Off to the Cities, here it goes," she announced as she carted off her first crate of lettuce. She stacked it next to the driveway so it would be ready to load in their truck for the 5:00 A.M. drive to the farmer's market.

"What's the matter with wearing plain old overalls or shorts and a T-shirt?" Big Brother Billy asked. "No, *you've* got to wear some kind of costume. May I point out that it's not Halloween? Someone might mistake you for a walking pole bean."

"Pole bean!" A.R. responded. "I might also point out that if you ever put your nose into a book instead of putting your nose in my business, you'd happen to know that I'm straight out of Sir J.M. Barrie's *Peter Pan*. That's J! M! Barrie, Big Brother Billy. Like A! R! Smith."

"Aren't *you* the cranky one this morning!" Big Brother Billy said as he went about his business in the garden.

Oh, if only Big Brother Billy wouldn't act so much like a big brother, even though he *is* my big brother, A.R. thought. And why does this have to be 4529 County Road C? Why can't this be Never-Never Land?

And with that, A.R. spread her arms out as if to take flight. She ran in a zigzag line, bobbing and weaving and jumping over the rows of lettuce to get to the next crate.

"I can fly! I can fly!" She repeated over and over.

And she did look as if she could almost fly as her cape flew out behind her.

Big Brother Billy smiled at his little sister. He didn't tell her so, but he was amused by her imagination. Just that morning, A.R. was demonstrating how to tell if an egg is raw or hard-boiled.

"Simple," she had explained. "Just spin the egg on its side. The hard-boiled egg spins faster than the raw one."

With that, A.R. gave both eggs a good twist. *Plop!* A cool and slimy egg was running down A.R.'s leg.

"I guess the yolk's on you," said Big Brother Billy as he gobbled down his chocolate-chip cinnamon bagel with peanut butter.

Mom was ready to laugh until she saw how embarrassed her daughter looked. She handed A.R. a paper towel to wipe off the yolk from her leg, and she brought over more towels to clean up the floor.

But A.R. was not interested in acknowledging a failure. She whacked the hard-boiled egg against the table and practically swallowed it whole. A.R. had something to prove. Science would triumph at that morning's breakfast table. A.R. was not going to let a little mess get in the way.

Still chewing her mouthful of egg, she began her experiment of the morning. "Please note, lady—," she paused and then looked at her brother, "and gentleman. I will demonstrate how raisins dance."

A.R. walked across the kitchen and retrieved a glass from the cupboard as well as a bottle of seltzer water from the refrigerator. She went back to the cupboard and got a handful of raisins.

"First, I fill a glass with seltzer water, like so. Then I drop a few raisins into the glass. Watch them dance!"

Then, to impress her audience, A.R. drank her experiment. After that, she disappeared upstairs and got ready for the day.

An hour later, A.R.'s flight around the garden and the terrific heat (the day's temperature was once again on its way to 110 degrees) churned up the hard-boiled egg, the seltzer water, and the raisins.

Her stomach started to rumble. Big Brother Billy saw his sister in pain. Her face was a paler shade of the green in her cape. He came to her aid.

"Sit down," he instructed her. Sitting down wasn't hard, since she was already kneeling on the ground.

"I'll get you some water." He went over to get the hose and offered A.R. a drink of water.

"I'm fine," she said weakly. And she took the hose and let the cool water trickle on her lips.

Then Big Brother Billy walked with her to the house and saw A.R. to her room.

Their father was out in the field. He was almost finished planting the soybeans. When Pappy saw Billy approaching, he turned down the opera he was listening to and shut off the cultivator. Billy told him what had happened, and Pappy went to the house to see his daughter. He sat on the edge of her bed and put a cold washcloth on her head.

"Are you all right, sweetest heart?" he called to her, using the pet name he saved for sympathetic moments.

"I just want to sleep," answered A.R.

"You do that. When Mom comes home from work, she'll look in on you. I'll give her a call." He pulled the shades down and left.

A.R.'s mother was the Kindbrae Postmaster. The post office was open Monday through Saturday until 12:30 P.M. And not a minute later!

At 12:37 P.M., A.R.'s mom was at her daughter's bedside. A.R. had been staring up at the glow-in-the-dark solar system pasted on the ceiling of her room.

A.R. was deep in thought. "Mom?" she asked. "Is

22

it possible to throw up in outer space? You can't throw down. Everything just floats. It's just weightless."

"What?" Mom was puzzled. This was not the question of a sick child.

In sickness or in health, A.R.'s thoughts, as well as her imagination, took flight.

Chapter 3

Kindbrae Goes to the Dogs

Right after the last of the Fourth of July fireworks lit up the sky over Drie Lake, Kindbrae began to clean up and dress up for "Those Good Old Days." Around the world, countries, cities, and towns put aside days to celebrate. The U.S. has the Fourth of July. France has Bastille Day. Boston has Patriot's Day. One of Kindbrae's neighboring towns celebrates Sauerkraut Days. Another celebrates Chicken Days. Kindbrae celebrates Those Good Old Days.

Those Good Old Days was a day founded by Lloyd Meisterteister, Sr., the original and first Official Town Historian of Kindbrae. He founded Those Good Old Days to celebrate his true love—history. As he would tell the town council, of which he was the head, "Ah, history, it's a story well told. And we're the ones to tell it." And each year, Kindbrae, MN, told the story, always in their own way.

Those Good Old Days was scheduled for the

second week of July, and would end with a big pageant and all-day picnic on Saturday. No matter what was happening in the fields, people took off for Those Good Old Days. People skipped their chores. They even hired others to take their fruits and vegetables to the farmer's market. All of Kindbrae got to live a life of yesterday.

The weather had behaved itself on the Fourth. It was a picture-perfect day of blue sky and sunshine. The next day, however, it began to rain.

Most kids don't look forward to rainy summer days. For A.R., however, they were almost like a holiday. A rainy day meant that she didn't have to work in the garden. Flo and Lloyd knew it meant that A.R. would come by the Kindbrae General Store and Cafe first thing in the morning.

Just as day followed night, one thing was sure—A.R. visited the Kindbrae General Store and Cafe on a daily basis to report in. On days when she had to work on the farm, she would come by for a midday report. She might try out some new candy they got in. Then she'd go help her mother close up the post office.

After that, mother and daughter would ride their

bicycles the three-quarters of a mile from town back to the farm. It was during those moments that A.R. got most of her news. And the next day, she'd tell Lloyd every last detail—who, what, when, and where.

In addition to everything that made up the 24 hours within her own day, A.R. filled Lloyd in on everything her mother Joyce would hear at the post office. Since mom talked to everyone who came in to pick up mail, she knew all about people's comings and goings in and around town. A.R. would, in turn, pass the information on to Lloyd.

"Your visits are a real contribution to history," Lloyd once told her. "Without them I wouldn't know half the hearsay that contributes to the accuracy of my reports as Official Town Historian."

"My junior journalist," Lloyd called her. And A.R. was proud of her title. It was one job she thought she carried out with responsibility.

That day the rain didn't seem to dampen the spirits of anyone else in town, either. By 7:00 A.M. on the morning of the fifth of July, Flo and Lloyd had the extra-big coffeepot and the two small coffeepots perking. By 7:23 A.M., Flo was up on a ladder out in front of the Kindbrae General Store and Cafe. She was straightening and adjusting and making sure the red, white, and blue bunting that was draped across the porch of the store was just so. The Good Old Days Decorating Committee was scheduled to arrive at 7:45, and Flo wanted to get a head start on decorating. More importantly, she wanted to get the multicolored twinkle lights in place before the committee arrived. They'd be sure to offer their two or three cents' worth on what she was doing. She could hear them now:

"Just a little lower on the right."

"Don't crisscross the middle row."

Flo was just about ready to hang the last string of lights over the bunting when she heard A.R.

"Good morning, Flo. I've never seen the Cafe's dining deck look so gorgeous!" said A.R.

"Aarf," Troxund the dachshund yapped in agreement a couple of times. This set up a chain reaction.

Scooter, Flo and Lloyd's pitbull, recognized Troxund's bark and started yelping in excitement inside the store, "Growl, woof, woof, woof."

By this time, Lily Sue's dog, Skip, began to yip and yap in a very ornery fashion. Skip, too, recognized Troxund's bark. Skip was a miniature Doberman. You'd think a Doberman would have a scary bark, but not Skip. Skip's yip and yap sounded like a smoke detector when the battery is running low.

"I'm going to get these lights up just so before anyone gets here. Look," Flo said as she looked down Main Street, "the morning is already beginning to lighten up." In fact the morning light *was* beginning to blink. But it wasn't coming from the sun or from the multicolored twinkle lights. The light came from Dr. Troxler's pick-up truck. Not from the headlights or taillights either, but from inside the truck. In the passenger's seat, Dr. Troxler had a mask propped up with eyes that blinked on and off. Blanche the dachshund was also in the front seat.

On the first Halloween when he came to town as the new veterinarian, Dr. Troxler rigged up the blinking mask as an addition to the costume he wore as the Phantom of the Kindbrae Grand Ole Opry. Dr. Troxler introduced his passenger by pointing to the blinking mask and saying, "Meet my main man."

On his way home from the Halloween party at The Kindbrae General Store and Cafe, he glanced at the blinking mask. And the mask glanced back at him. "Cheered me up," he said later. And the kids—at least those under nine years old—thought it was the funniest thing any adult could ever do.

After he bought a new truck, the mask still rode

beside him. And on rainy days and holidays, he always made sure the lights were blinking. It made him and the kids happy. His mission was to help *all* of Kindbrae's citizens.

Dr. Troxler made sure stray animals found good homes. One time he had to find a home for a mother dachshund that was ready to give birth. When the litter came, Dr. Troxler kept one of the puppies and he convinced the Smiths, among others, to take another.

"Hey, our puppy's eyes blink just like the mask in your truck," Mr. Smith remarked. "Maybe we should call our new dachshund 'Troxler.'"

"Call him Troxund! It rhymes with dachshund," shouted A.R. The name stuck: Troxund the dachshund.

The days between the Fourth of July and Those Good Old Days were always filled with plenty of excitement. However, this year's excitement began to pick up even more when Troxund heard his sister Blanche start barking. She was still sitting in the front seat of the pick-up truck.

With a mighty yank, Troxund pulled free of the leash that A.R. was holding. Just as he did, his back paw got stuck in a loop of the twinkle lights that Flo was stringing up. In his continued excitement, Troxund ran around the ladder that was holding Flo. The string of twinkle lights tangled around the ladder. Troxund pulled the ladder, which came out from under Flo, leaving her hanging on to the red, white, and blue bunting. Meanwhile, Troxund kept on running to the truck. Trailing behind him was the ladder and the twinkle lights.

"The lights!" yelled Flo, still clinging to the bunting.

Lloyd heard this from inside the store and thought Flo wanted him to turn on the lights for a test. He plugged them in. The lights twinkled across the deck of the cafe all the way to Dr. Troxler's pick-up truck.

The eyes of the mask looked on, still blinking.

Flo had not paid attention to what kind of twinkle lights she had purchased. It was not until Lloyd threw the switch that Flo realized she was using musical, multicolored twinkle lights. As the lights were turned on, they started to play "Jingle Bells." The sounds of Christmas filled the air. By this time, all the dogs in town were barking, yipping, yapping, howling, and growling, except for Scooter. He suddenly got bored by it all and went back to his blanket in the canned goods section of the Kindbrae General Store and Cafe, presumably to wait it out.

Suddenly the bunting ripped and Flo tumbled two-and-a-half feet into a pile of inflated $6.99 wading pools displayed outside the General Store—landing softly and gently.

By 8:22 A.M., the decorating committee had seen to it that Flo was OK. Then they had their coffee and sweet rolls. It was time to begin their work in earnest. The committee decided to keep up the ten flags that had lined Main Street for the Fourth of July. This year, as every year, the decorating committee discussed and agreed to hang baskets filled with red plastic begonias and trailing ivy from each of the nine lampposts and three telephone poles in town.

Then they began to help Flo put back the red, white, and blue bunting and restring the twinkle lights.

"Just a little lower on the right," said Violet Jeffrey, Lily Sue's mother.

"Don't crisscross the middle row," said Dr. Mel Beck, the middle school principal.

Some things just never change, thought Flo.

Chapter 4

History Takes the Stage

Teachers who had the summer off were a big help with Those Good Old Days. Ms. Delphinium Beck (A.R.'s third-grade teacher) donated over 300 blue and pink carnations that she had folded from blue and pink facial tissues. She had strung them together to make garlands to hang on each of the six trees that stood in tubs that lined Main Street.

The sixth of July, although less eventful, was still damp and rainy. By 7:33 A.M., A.R. was peddling her bike to the General Store with Troxund in tow. On the way she passed the trees. The tissue paper carnations sagged with moisture. A.R.'s spirits were sagging as well.

"Don't look so sad," Flo said as she looked sympathetically at A.R. "OK, so the decorating got off on a bad foot. But look around. Kindbrae looks beautiful. And I showed everyone just how sturdy those wading pools are."

"Oh, *that!*" A.R. responded. Actually, A.R. thought it was all kind of funny, but she couldn't say that to Flo. "No, it's something else. Flo, no one wants to be my brother!"

"What? Billy has disowned you?" Flo asked as she went about crocheting the crown she was going to wear in the Those Good Old Days' Pageant. She had decided to go as Princess Kaiulani, the last princess of Hawaii. Flo had a great love for our 50th state, even though she'd never been there.

Her entire costume, including the bows on her shoes, was going to be crocheted. Not only that, she had crocheted a blanket and leggings for Shawn, Bathtub's mother. Shawn was to pull the wagon in which Flo was going to ride with Bathtub. Shawn's blanket was lime green and yellow to contrast with Flo's plum purple and orange cape. The bows on Flo's shoes, however, were lime green and yellow. Shawn's leggings were plum purple and orange, which would match the ribbon braided through Shawn's tail. Flo thought of it as her masterpiece.

Ms. Beck had been busy, too. She had made all new carnations. This time she sprayed them with shellac so they'd be waterproof.

"Rain can't ruin them. And we can use them from year to year," she pointed out proudly when she brought them in to show Flo and Lloyd.

When A.R. saw Ms. Beck, she burst into tears.

"What's the matter?" asked Ms. Beck.

"No one wants to be my brother," sobbed A.R.

"Did Billy disown you?"

"That's just what I asked," said Flo.

"No, I haven't been disowned," answered A.R. "I'm planning on being Orville Wright. But what's one Wright brother without the other? Who could be more important in the Pageant of History than the two people who invented the airplane?

"I asked Big Brother Billy, but he's got his own idea for a costume. I asked Pappy if he would shave his beard so he could be Wilbur. 'No way,' he told me. 'I grew it so I could be Abraham Lincoln.'" A.R.'s voice trailed off in thought.

"Mr. Meisterteister?" she said in a suddenly cheery voice.

"Yes, Miss Aida Rose Smith?" he responded.

Lloyd Meisterteister knew that A.R. wanted something. She called him Mr. Meisterteister either when she wanted something or when she had done something wrong. "Mr. Meisterteister, would you play Orville or Wilbur? I'll let you be whichever brother you want to be."

Lloyd thought deeply before he spoke. "You know

that as the Official Town Historian, I'm in charge of reporting on the event for the newspaper. Furthermore, I have to judge the presentations. The most historical gets a prize. If we were the Wright brothers, we'd be the most historical, of course. But then people would accuse me of not being fair. I have to stay true to both of my sacred offices—the Official Town Historian and the Pageant Judge.

"Besides, this year I have my new video camera. I don't want to miss a minute of the celebration. What about Lily Sue?" Mr. Meisterteister asked.

"I've already asked her. Then we got into an argument." A.R. proceeded to tell Lloyd all about it.

"Do you know what she said to me when I asked her? She said, 'The Wright brothers? They'll call us the Wrong sisters.' I didn't think that was funny at all."

"Well, you know the old saying: 'Two wrongs don't make a right.' Looks like Lily Sue thinks two Wrongs don't make two Wrights," said Lloyd.

"But we all know that two Wrights can make an airplane!" A.R. responded, as she forgot her disappointment for a moment.

A.R. took a seat in the table section of the Kindbrae General Store and Cafe, where she sat thinking about the pageant. Troxund lay curled up at her feet.

Pappy had already helped her make a plane according to her design. They took two curtain rods and attached them to the seat of her old bicycle. They attached a pulley to the center of the handlebars. Then they strung nylon stockings from each end of the outstretched curtain rods to the center pulley. When A.R. pulled the stockings through the pulley, the curtain rods moved up and down. At one-foot intervals, they bent coat hangers around the curtain rods to make ribs for their wings. They covered the wings with wrapping paper. Tiny Sybrandt donated some leftover silver paint from the Kindbrae Town Dump and Recycling Center and they used that to paint the wings.

A.R. was on her way to capturing first prize. All she needed was a Wilbur. She had a great costume and a terrific airplane, but no one to march with her.

If only La, her grandmother, were here, A.R. thought. I bet she'd even wear a fake mustache. She'd make sure that we'd look just like Orville and Wilbur.

La was short for her family name, Lacracia. La never wanted anyone to call her "Grandmother" or "Grandma."

"Call me 'La,'" she insisted. "In my head, I'm too young to be called 'Grandma.'" That didn't matter to A.R. Just saying the name 'La' felt good in her mouth.

There were two things in life that A.R. dreamed of being. One was to be an astronaut. The other was to be just like her grandmother. For La, every day was an adventure. Everything had a story. A.R. Loved La— and that's *Loved*, spelled with a capital *L*.

"Oh, Troxund," she said as she lifted him up in her arms. "Do you want to be a Wright brother?" And then genius struck. She got on her bike and rode over to Trixie O'Rourke's neighboring farm. The O'Rourkes had five-month-old twins, so maybe Trixie would have what A.R. decided she needed.

"Come in. Sit down." Trixie invited A.R. in and had her sit on the old couch in the living room.

"Trixie, will you keep a secret?"

"Depends, honey."

Then A.R. went about explaining her problem of the missing Wright brother to Trixie.

Trixie interrupted the tale of woe. "No! I'm definitely not going to be your brother. I have new twins to take care of. Raising Luca and raising Kane is work enough."

"I wasn't thinking that. I just need to borrow a baby bonnet. I need to color it black," A.R. added sheepishly. "I need to make a pilot's hat for Troxund, but don't tell anyone. I want it to be a surprise."

"Well, that's not a problem. We must've received

ten baby bonnets as shower presents and Baby Luca and Baby Kane have outgrown every one. Such big boys. Let's go dig one up for you."

A.R. thanked Trixie, raced back home, took a felt pen from her collection, and madly started to color the blue bonnet black. She put it on Troxund. He tried to shake it off, but he got used to it. It was a little more of a problem to fit him with swim goggles that were supposed to be flight glasses.

"So who do *you* want to be, Troxund—Wilbur or Orville?" A.R. asked. "Yes, I think you make a very good-looking Orville," she concluded, looking at her new brother.

The days before the pageant flew by. On the big day, breakfast at the Smith family's house, and probably throughout town, was eaten quickly. The line-up for the grand entrance began at 9:00 A.M.

"Pappy, you look so handsome," said A.R. when she saw her father with his beard combed and wearing a high-collar shirt and a black coat with tails.

"Aarf," Troxund agreed. Both Pappy and Mrs. Smith thought Troxund looked so cute in his cap and the little silk scarf that A.R. tied around his neck.

Mr. Smith gave his wife a hug. "I'll be the most

handsome man in the pageant. Can't you close up the post office today?" Pappy asked.

"I couldn't get anyone to watch it," Mom said.

Billy came into the room and looked at his sister and Troxund. He started laughing. "Who are you two—Snoopy and the Red Baron?"

His comment was too much for A.R. She had worked so hard. She began to cry.

"Come on, Billy. That's not nice," Mom scolded. "Apologize."

"I'm sorry, Baron—er—Aida Rose."

A.R.'s tears turned to sobs. Big Brother Billy hightailed it out of there to join his friends. Her mom wiped away A.R.'s tears.

"I'm going to stay home and watch the Exploration Channel. I don't care about any dumb old pageant," A.R. said between sobs.

"That doesn't sound like our A.R. Smith," said Pappy. "Besides, the satellite dish is broken. You know that."

"I forgot." No television. No pageant. A.R. was beginning to rethink her sadness.

"You take Orville and Wilbur down to the town hall, Pappy," Mom said. "There are people from as far away as the Cities coming to see the pageant."

A.R.'s mom and dad managed to get a little smile

out of their daughter. Pappy led her off as Mom sat down at the table and stared out the window, watching her family leave.

Busses full of band members arrived in town.

The local radio station, KUTE, set up a remote broadcast facility outside the Kindbrae General Store. They provided live coverage for the entire one hour and 12 minutes in which the great figures of history marched and strutted their way up Main Street and into the town hall.

For the first time, the entire event was recorded by Lloyd Meisterteister on his new palm-sized video camera that Flo had given him for their 42nd wedding anniversary. Lloyd thought that customers might come into the Kindbrae General Store and Cafe and take the tape out on loan. They'd see for themselves what a dazzling spectacle Those Good Old Days really is. Lloyd imagined that the Kindbrae General Store and Cafe was on its way to becoming a media center.

The participants assembled down by the Kindbrae Town Dump and Recycling Center. Those Good Old Days was billed as "the greatest indoor pageant in the Midwest." For years it had been held in a field at the end of town. But for five years in a row the pageant was washed out by rain. After that, Lloyd made arrangements with the school board to hold the pageant at the high school gym even if it meant that only one band and two floats or three wagons could come through at a time.

The Town Dump and Recycling Center wasn't the most glamorous of beginnings, but it was the largest open space people could gather in before heading up to the high school. Besides, the marchers were welcome to take things from the pile marked "Still Good After All These Years." You could never tell what last-minute prop or costume addition they might need. And Tiny Sybrandt was ready with suggestions.

The pageant committee had the marchers set up by categories. They got in line behind marching bands that came from as far away as Grahamville, Haversville, Goldsville, and Villesville. From the dump they would proceed uptown. Then, beginning with the dinosaurs, participants would enter the hall, parade around the room, and pause before the judge's stand.

Ms. Delphinium Beck, A.R.'s teacher, came as Sarah, a pioneer woman from her favorite book, *Sarah, Plain and Tall.* She was tall, about six feet, but she was hardly plain.

"I think she's one of the most beautiful women in the world," Lily Sue said to her friend A.R.

Lily Sue and her mother both wore long dresses and bonnets. Mrs. Jeffrey carried books, while Lily Sue carried a writing slate. At Lily Sue's insistence, mother and daughter were a pioneer teacher and her student.

Big Brother Billy wore a discarded TV box from the Kindbrae Town Dump and Recycling Center. He painted it black, cut a hole in the top of the TV box, and cut two holes in the sides so he could stick his head and arms through the holes. Tiny Sybrandt gave

him an old television antenna and Billy placed it on his head. Billy walked around waving from inside the box. To anyone who wanted to know, he explained that he was the first television set.

Lloyd got everything on tape. He was proud of Flo as she rode around the gym, waving regally to the crowd. Bathtub sat next to her as Shawn pulled the wagon in her crocheted blanket, leggings, and braid. A sign on the wagon read, "Princess Kaiulani of Hawaii and Her Pony, Sponsored by the Kindbrae General Store and Cafe."

Maybe the pageant didn't read like a history book, but it sure had enthusiasm. The committee decided long ago against arguing who could or could not be in the pageant. Everyone got in. They even let the animals into the gym for just that one day. Lloyd convinced everyone that the pageant itself was history. It was history in the making.

On the back of Dr. Troxler's truck was a replica of the Mount Rushmore National Monument. He had used papier-mâché and plastic foam to sculpt the heads of the four presidents. Trouble was, it was too big to get into the building, so the committee made an exception and judged it outside the gym.

"Lincoln's head looks just like Pappy's," said A.R.

Big Glenn marched as Wild Bill Hickock. His

daughter, Tammy, was Annie Oakley. There were marchers from Northville, Southville, Eastville, Westville, and Centerville. The Eastville Sew and Grow 4-H Club made historical dioramas using dolls, toys, and a combination of clay, twigs, and clumps of sod. Each diorama depicted a different scene of farm life on the prairie—from pioneer times to the present. You had to get up close to see everything, but it was worth it. Each of the dioramas was mounted on a skateboard, which they pulled around the gym. Similarly, the Boy Scouts and Girl Scouts rigged up hoops over supermarket carts and covered them with blankets. They had wheeled them up Main Street as a wagon train heading westward.

The Southville Dancing Bears followed them. A Southville farmer, Myles Long, was famous for raising sheepdogs. He dressed them in tutus and bow ties and marched them in most of the parades around the state. For this Pageant, he named them the Southville Dancing Bears, after an act in the first circus that came to Minnesota. Even less historical, but well disciplined, were the lifeguards from the county pool. They came as the Surfboard Marching Drill Squad. Every pageant should have a drill squad, and they filled the bill.

Roberta Bobbe led the Southwest Tap Dance and

Baton School. Most of the kids were so young that several mothers had to march alongside them. They were needed to pick up the batons if the kids dropped them and help if the kids needed to get out of line because they got tired of marching.

Bob Bobbe was dressed as Thomas Edison. Other people came dressed as George Washington, Sitting Bull, and Florence Nightingale. Dillon Dimock, Big Brother Billy's friend, came as a Dr. Seuss character.

A.R. had to wait awhile before it was her turn. The Wright brothers were part of the last section, Modern History. She was playing with Troxund as she looked up.

"Mom!" she yelled.

Mrs. Smith had borrowed Big Brother Billy's black cargo pants and her husband's aviator sunglasses. She was wearing Pappy's old leather bomber jacket that he'd had since his college days.

"Oh, honey, I was finishing my coffee when La called and we got to talking. Your grandmother got me thinking that I shouldn't miss Those Good Old Days."

Mom continued. "Then I got to remembering your dad's old bomber jacket. And here I am." She pulled out a tissue and wiped beads of sweat off her forehead.

"But what about the post office?" A.R. asked.

"We've got a *T-rex* in charge. Mel Beck left the front of the march just as soon as he finished leading the Junior High School Dinosaur Kazoo Band. I called him up before he left this morning and he agreed to come over just as he reached the town hall.

"Come on, Wilbur—or is it Orville?—let's march."

Mother, daughter, dog, and airplane proudly joined the pageant. A.R. floated as if she were one of those balloons that she saw each year on TV in the Thanksgiving Day Parade.

Just as everyone was allowed to appear in the pageant, everyone received a blue ribbon. Although Lloyd liked to play up his importance as judge of the pageant, there were no losers in this town.

"This year, as in previous years, we have a tie for the Best Band, the Best Float, and the Most Historical Costume," Lloyd announced at the end of the pageant. Since the judges are unable to decide who is number one, we're awarding each of you a beautiful first-prize blue ribbon." Lloyd just couldn't hurt anyone's feelings.

"Everyone is a winner," he declared. Everyone cheered and came up to collect his or her blue ribbon.

A.R. came home a double winner: She had a ribbon for Most Historical Costume, and she had the best mom in Kindbrae.

Chapter 5

Traveling to Minn-plis and Sit Paul

After Those Good Old Days, life around Kindbrae, MN, pretty much settled down to business as usual. Everyone thought it was the best Those Good Old Days that Kindbrae ever celebrated. But this was also the busiest part of the growing season. There was work to be done. *Responsibility.* There was that word again.

When A.R. and Big Brother Billy weren't working in the garden, there were other things to do around the farm. Animals to feed. Fences to mend (Big Brother Billy's responsibility). Collecting eggs. Feeding and watering the chickens (A.R.'s responsibilities). And once a week, they'd go off to the farmer's market in the Cities.

"They're *two* cities," A.R. once argued, but that argument went nowhere. Anyone who did not live in

Minneapolis, St. Paul, or the surrounding suburbs thought of them as one: the Cities.

Being nine years old added more responsibilities to A.R.'s growing list. This year A.R. was expected to help out at the farmer's market. Big Brother Billy had to go every week. A.R. went every other week. But next year she'd become a full-time employee of the Smith Family's Garden and Farm Stand and make the weekly trip to the market.

For A.R., going to market was hardly a problem. She had already made friends at the farmer's market. She liked weighing the produce, making change, and talking to the customers. She smiled proudly when people admired her hand-lettered sign, "Straight from the garden to your home." She decorated it with drawings of cabbages encircled with rings to look like Saturn, and carrots that looked like rocket ships.

On Friday everything had to be picked and crated, and the flowers arranged in bouquets. A.R. had stopped dressing up for the time being. She looked pretty much like any nine-year-old, except that she was wearing one of her prized possessions, her well-worn cap printed with the letters NASA. The letters meant "National Aeronautics and Space Administration."

It was a cool summer, so the Smiths were still able

to bring lettuce and mixed greens to the market. Once each of the crates was filled, out came the hose and A.R. watered down the greens with funny-sounding names like mizuna, arugula, and Swiss chard.

"Whoever thought up the names of these vegetables?" she asked Big Brother Billy.

"They sound more like names of towns in Europe than they do vegetables, don't they?" Big Brother Billy responded as he yanked up the beets in his part of the garden. "Lettuce fly off to Arugula," he joked.

"I'd rather zoom off to Mizuna," A.R. added. "Lettuce. Oh, I get it. That's funny, Billy."

For a minute he was just plain Billy instead of Big Brother Billy. Sometimes he acted just like a friend and they'd pass the time swapping riddles.

A.R. had a new one she made up that morning. "My body is long. My head is bristly. What am I?"

Billy thought for a moment. "I don't know. Give me another clue."

"I live in the bathroom." There was a pause. "OK, I'll tell you. A toothbrush," A.R. laughed.

"Well, you've been busy thinking this morning, haven't you?" Billy replied just as some birds flew overhead, giving him an idea. "I've got one for you. Why do birds fly south?"

Pappy was coming to check on the kids' progress

and overheard Billy. "Because it's too far to walk," he answered before A.R. had a chance to even think of an answer.

"No fair," she said, knowing that Pappy was the king of riddles in the Smith family. He could always stump them with a real brainteaser.

"Here's a really hard one. What's black and white and red all over?" asked Pappy.

"Oh, that's easy—a newspaper! We all know that one," answered A.R.

"No, a sunburned cow," Pappy replied. "And you're going to be sunburned, too. Did you put on sunscreen?"

"Oh, Pappy," they responded in unison as Pappy handed them a tube of sunscreen.

Billy slapped it on and then went to pick the rest of the beets. *Clunk!* went the spade. *Clunk!*

Billy shouted, "I think I hit buried treasure. Pay dirt!" He continued digging and pulled out the can of an old grease gun. He kept on pulling. The can was screwed onto a fence post with what looked like two plywood fins nailed to the base of the post.

"What's this?" he asked.

"Oh, that," said A.R. in a matter-of-fact voice. "It's a space capsule I buried last year. Do you like the rocket ship design?"

"Let's open it," said Big Brother Billy.

"Don't! It's for future generations to find out about us. I put my final report card in there and my diary, too."

Too late. Big Brother Billy had already unscrewed the grease can and was pulling out a damp and tattered book and some papers. It looked like something from the compost heap.

"A little damp," said Big Brother Billy.

"Oops," said A.R. "I guess I need to work out my design."

"Maybe there's a market for space capsules fresh from the garden. Should we take it to the farmer's market?" Pappy remarked.

A.R. didn't look too pleased.

As the Smiths drove to the Cities, they passed distant towns, fields, and grain elevators that looked like the towers of ancient castles or cathedrals. It was a day kissed by sunshine, Pappy thought, and that meant it would be a good day for customers.

A.R. slept most of the way. When she wasn't sleeping, she would lay back in the passenger's seat and gaze at the passing countryside. Row after row of soybeans and corn grew in the fields. The many rows of plants whizzed past like the spinning spokes of a bicycle wheel and she felt that she was flying by. A.R. liked that.

The highway sign read "Minneapolis–St. Paul 50 miles." "Fifty miles," Pappy announced. "Fifty miles until Minn-plis and Sit Paul." When he was young and learning to read, Big Brother Billy would show off his new skills by reading the signs and billboards. When he saw the sign for Minneapolis and St. Paul, he puzzled over it and sounded it out, "Minn-plis— Sit Paul." It became a family joke.

The last 50 miles seemed endless. A.R. had an urge to ask, "Are we there yet?" but she didn't dare. There was a driving rule. In years past, either Billy or A.R. would ask the question way too often. At least once every 25 miles. So Pappy and Mom introduced a rule. Anyone who asked that question had to put a quarter into the driving fund. No one asked the question anymore.

Fifty miles. Twenty miles. The skyscrapers of downtown Minneapolis came into view. They took the road that led them around Minneapolis and to the St. Paul Regional Farmer's Market. By 7:00 A.M. they reached their exit. In a few minutes the Smiths were backing their truck into their stall, number 402.

Other farmers began pulling up to their stalls. The market began to unfold with sounds, colors, and aromas. Live chickens and ducks in cages squawked. Trucks were unloaded. Stands were being set up. Some farmers took great pride in their stands, carefully arranging the radishes, onions, scallions, cheese, eggs, honey, and flowers in every color of the rainbow. The farmer's market was a circus of colors and aromas.

One orchard set up their space with samples of fruit for the customers to taste and cold fruit juices to buy. Another stand had a huge coffee urn, which was heating up apple cider. Pappy went down to the food stand to get a cup of coffee. A.R. went along to get juice for herself and Big Brother Billy. Along the way they picked up fresh donuts from a stand selling baked goods.

"Hello, Roger. Hi, Mrs. Nelson. How was your ride to the Cities? Have much rain this week?" A.R. and Pappy greeted the other farmers. They had many friends at the market.

The children at the market had their own language, greeting each other with animal sounds from around the world.

"Um-moo," greeted Le Mai Nhu in Vietnamese, as if she were a cow.

"Ki-ki-ri-kí," Milo Reynoso said in Spanish, as he imitated a rooster crowing.

"Iiii iii," his younger sister, Elizabeth, chirped like a bird.

"Cock-a-doodle-doo," answered A.R.

Big Brother Billy stayed behind and finished unloading the truck. He was the fussy one in the family and believed that customers liked the look of what the Smiths sold as much as price and quality. He had an eye for both color and arrangement. If there were too many rows of green vegetables, he'd break up the pattern with a carefully arranged display of yellow summer squash. When he had everything arranged just the way he wanted it, he put up the signs that listed all the prices. For the final touch, Billy placed buckets of colorful snapdragons, bright spears of blue larkspur, poppies, and black-eyed Susans at each corner of the stand.

Pappy and A.R. came back to help get ready for the 8:00 opening of the market.

"Picture perfect," Pappy concluded.

"I think this zucchini is out of place," A.R. said as she pulled out the bottom-most zucchini in the pile.

One zucchini began to roll forward, then two, and pretty soon the whole pile was in motion, spilling onto the cement floor of the stall.

"Whoa," A.R. said, reaching her arms out to prevent the landslide of vegetables from rolling off the stand. Too late. A.R. stood like a statue surrounded by a pedestal of zucchini.

"Aida Rose!" Big Brother Billy screamed and charged toward his sister. Pappy played the referee between the two, holding them off from what could have turned nasty. But Billy was actually more concerned about how everything looked than he was in getting even with his sister.

"Help me!" he demanded. So A.R. started gingerly placing the zucchini back in place.

Right after lunch, business usually started to slow down at the farmer's market, but today wasn't going to slow down for A.R. and her friends. A.R. went to get Thien Van Nhu and his sister, Le Mai. They had been invited to Milo Reynoso's tenth birthday party.

"Moo!" A.R. belted out loudly.

"Guau guau," Thien barked like a dog to show off his Spanish.

"Guau guau into the truck, Thien," said Mr. Nhu.

"Let's unload the rest of the bok choy."

The Nhus grew several kinds of vegetables that were especially popular with the Chinese, Laotian, and Vietnamese people who shopped at the market. There were herbs, long seedless cucumbers, boiled soybeans they called *edamame*, cassava, and white sweet potatoes.

"What's that?" cried Thien.

Two bright, marble-sized eyes stared at them from the rear corner of the truck. Chewed up carrots, greens, and beets lay in piles like confetti. And then they noticed a black-striped tail.

Out waddled a raccoon that looked around and then scurried down the aisle.

"A raccoon!" screamed a customer.

"Stand aside, children," announced Mr. Reynoso. "This is a job for adults. Let's go." In pursuit, he stepped on a tomato that squirted up toward Mrs. Reynoso's face.

"Good start," she said.

Pretty soon a crowd was after the raccoon. It scampered from one side of the aisle to the other, upending stand after stand. Soon the market was in a hubbub. The customers seemed amused. And so was the raccoon as it raced around overturning baskets and carts. Vegetables and fruits spilled all over the place.

Then the animal hid behind a big bushel basket and poked its head out from its hiding place. Someone tossed the raccoon an ear of corn, which it picked up with its front paws and started to eat.

"Oh, how cute," A.R. remarked. And all the children agreed.

The adults, however, did not seem amused.

"We have to catch it!" someone yelled.

In no time, a small posse surrounded the raccoon. Mrs. Nelson threw a basket over it.

Mr. Nhu quickly followed with an empty crate he used as a makeshift cage.

"Shhh, everyone," he said, trying to calm the onlookers so the raccoon wouldn't scare anyone more than it had. Mr. Nhu placed a handful of carrots into the crate. And then he carefully placed the crate next to the trapped raccoon and inched up to the bushel basket. As he hoped, the raccoon crawled into the crate, and Mr. Nhu quickly brought down the lid.

For the time being, the raccoon had a new home for its ride back to their farm, where Mr. Nhu would let it go in the countryside.

"Did you invite your raccoon friend to the party?" Mr. Reynoso joked. "I don't know if we have enough food." But there was more than enough food: tamales, tacos, soda pop, and a large sheet cake decorated with soccer balls. On it was printed in thick blue icing, *"¡Feliz cumpleaños, Milo!"* Happy Birthday, Milo!

Pappy provided the music. He asked several of the farmers to turn on their truck radios to the same Spanish station, creating a mini-concert. He first tried to persuade them to tune in the Saturday opera broadcast, but that suggestion was about as welcome as ice cubes during a snowstorm.

Milo's entire family was there. In addition to his mother, father, and younger brother and sister, his relatives from the Cities arrived—aunts, uncles, cousins, and even his grandmother—his *abuela*.

The kids gobbled down the food. They knew what was next. The *piñata!* From the rafter overhead hung a large paper figure in the shape of a duck. The children knew that it held candy and other surprises that they would share.

"You're up first, Milo," Mr. Reynoso directed as he blindfolded his son and gave him a stick to hit the *piñata*.

"Wait!" shouted his Uncle Ivan. Then he came over to twirl his nephew around.

"One! Two! Three . . ." Everyone joined in counting to ten—one spin for each year.

"Yeah!" Everyone cheered and laughed as Milo swung at the *piñata*, giving it one good hit, then another.

Milo was the birthday boy so he got four turns. But that didn't make hitting it any easier. A rope slung over the rafter of the stall held the *piñata*, which Mrs. Reynoso would raise and lower so it was never in the same place.

The children lined up for their turn, from little Ivana, age four, to Big Brother Billy.

The children's voices rang out with directions. "To the right! Up! Take two steps! Over there!"

The *piñata* had sustained more than a dozen hits, but it still was in one piece.

"Let me at it!" demanded *Abuela*. "Give me that stick," she said, moving into the center of the action.

"First the blindfold," Mr. Reynoso reminded her. *Abuela* had many years of practice. *Wham!* She gave it a swipe as if she were hitting a home run. Out poured candy and gifts of little plastic horses, stickers, whistles, yo-yos, nuts, and candy shaped like fruits wrapped in shiny pink, yellow, and orange papers.

The candy showered the stall just as another group of children was walking by. They looked nothing like the kids at the party. They looked more like little adults in their uniforms: identical khaki shorts, sneakers, and polo shirts. Each one was carrying a clipboard. The shirts were embroidered with each child's name and the words, "Space Cadet Camp." They all looked very serious.

A.R. was scrambling for her share of the gifts and candy, but looked up as this group of invaders came her way.

One of the girls was talking a mile a minute with her partner.

"I think radishes are too small to take into space. They'll just float all over the cabin. I know we need to eat vegetables on our voyage. Maybe we can . . . " her voice trailed off.

A.R. stared in disbelief. Who *were* these kids? Were they really talking about space travel? And that girl's voice sounds familiar. A.R. looked closer. Then she noticed the girl's name: Becky. It was her old friend, *Snuckergans*.

"Becky Lambordini!" she shouted.

Becky looked puzzled. She quit talking to her partner.

"Aida Rose Smith?" she asked with a huge smile beaming across her face. "What a surprise!"

"They call me A.R. now," A.R. informed her as they hugged.

Becky began talking again, practically without taking a breath. She quickly told her cadet friends who A.R. was. "This is my friend from when I lived in the country. I haven't seen her for two years. We used to build spaceships together."

Then Becky told A.R. why she was at the market. "These are my friends from camp," she said, pointing to the children in uniform. "We're in Space Cadet Camp together. Our assignment is to come up with well-balanced meals that can be freeze-dried to take into space."

A.R. couldn't believe her ears.

Becky showed A.R. the form she was working on. A.R. recognized the food pyramid.

"Space Cadet Camp?" A.R. asked in amazement.

"Don't you watch the Exploration Channel?" asked Becky. "They sponsor a camp to train kids just like real astronauts are trained. We're in special housing at the university. And we take classes and everything. At the end of this week, we get to go into an antigravity chamber and float around just like astronauts do in outer space."

"Oh, Becky, how did you get to be so lucky? That's my dream." Then A.R. yelled to her father, "Pappy, Becky's going to Space Cadet Camp. Can you believe this? If our satellite dish wasn't broken, I would've known about Space Cadet camp."

"C'mon, cadets, we've got to get back to training school," the camp counselor interrupted.

"Here's my address." Becky ripped off a piece of paper from her clipboard. "Write me!"

The girls hugged. "For sure," said A.R.

Unlike most trips back to Kindbrae, A.R. didn't find herself falling off to sleep. She was wide awake, filled with daydreams, good food, and a sense of purpose.

She kept her daydreams to herself, but she did break her silence at one point. "Pappy, *Abuela* told me that she made the tamales. She called them *tamales en mole*. Did you know that *mole* is made with chocolate? Chocolate *tamales!* They didn't taste like chocolate."

"What did you think of the tacos?" Pappy asked.

"They're not like the ones Mom makes. They were good." Then she recited the names she learned. "*Taco de sesos, taco de lengua, taco de tripa.*"

"Hey guys. Remember, I've taken Spanish in school. That's tacos with brain meat, tacos with tongue, tacos with intestines," Big Brother Billy informed his family. "Not for me."

"Well, I thought they were delicious," A.R. said with a gulp. Then she looked at her father and moaned. "I think there's a giant living in my stomach."

CHAPTER 6

A.R.'s First Solo Flight

"Sorry the satellite dish can't be repaired yet," Pappy said as he reached for his second helping of green beans. "It won't be fixed until the repair guys are off strike."

A.R. wasn't listening. "I wrote Becky three days ago, and there's still no answer."

"Don't be so impatient. She's busy at space camp," Mom answered.

"I could probably be busy at Space Cadet Camp, too, if I had the Exploration Channel to watch," A.R. whined.

"Are we on planet Grumpy tonight?" Pappy asked.

"Not funny." A.R.'s voice trailed off as she headed for the kitchen door. Her last words could be heard from the yard. "I'm going to Lily Sue's, where there's a television set. With ninety channels," she added.

Fifteen minutes later, A.R. returned. The family

had gathered in the family room. Big Brother Billy's face was glued to a Web site on the computer screen.

"I forgot that Lily Sue went on vacation," A.R. said. "Everybody gets to go somewhere."

She slumped down on the sofa and stared at the blank TV screen.

"A penny for your thoughts," Pappy said from his chair across the room.

Silence.

"Fifty cents?"

"Ms. Smith, this is planet Earth to Voyager. Come in, Voyager," Pappy announced.

More silence.

"Ms. Smith, this is planet Earth. This is an emergency. We need a smile in order to continue our voyage." Pappy continued to try to reach A.R.

Still no response, but Pappy did make contact. An ever-so-slight smile crept over A.R.'s face.

Crack! From nowhere, thunder rumbled and a bolt of lightning lit the room. Troxund leaped into A.R.'s arms. Rain began pouring down.

"Ah, maybe tomorrow it will pour and we'll take the day off," Pappy said.

"Not with *my* luck," A.R. declared, inching her way back into her grumpy mood.

"Life isn't fair, is it?" asked Pappy, just as another

loud burst of thunder exploded in the sky.

"No, it isn't," A.R. sighed.

Troxund howled.

"I guess even Troxund agrees," Pappy concluded.

The next day arrived without any downpours. In fact, it was hazy, hot, and humid. A.R. worked in the garden as usual. And by midday—sure as you could set your clocks by her—she was in town for her daily visit to the Kindbrae General Store and Cafe and then to the post office to meet her mother.

"There's a letter for you," Mom said when A.R. came in.

La

Aida Rose Smith
4529 County Road C
Kindbrae, Minnesota 55400

"It must be from Becky. I knew she'd write," A.R. said.

"No, it's from La," Mom replied.

"La! Yippee!" A letter from La was even better than a letter from Becky Lambordini.

A.R. ripped open the envelope and a ticket fell out.

Dear Aida Rose,

I'm sorry you weren't home when I called. I was missing you terribly. But that was the morning of the big pageant in Kindbrae and you had more important things to do. How much I wish I could've seen you as a Wright brother. I hope you took pictures of the pageant.

I want to know all about it, so why not come to New York and tell me? I've already discussed it with your mom. You're old enough. With the flight crew's help, you can fly out here solo. And we'll fly back together. The ticket is your birthday present. Start packing!

Much love,
La

A.R. was already expecting her grandmother's summer visit. It was a tradition. But A.R. never dreamed she'd see La in New York first.

La visited Kindbrae every year by the tenth of

August, *La Notte de San Lorenzo*, the Night of Saint Lorenzo. The Night of the Shooting Stars.

Every year La would retell the story of this special night, each time a little bit differently.

"Keeps up the interest," she remarked.

"The Night of Saint Lorenzo," La began in her deep dramatic voice, "is the night when your dreams come true." La would be carried back to her own childhood and her parents' home in Italy. "Great-grandmother Nani would let us stay up late to watch the night sky. It seemed as if you could reach out and touch the Milky Way. It looked like a lace curtain spread against the evening sky. And if you saw a shooting star that night, all the people in Nani's village in Sicily believed that your dreams came true."

And there was some truth to the legend of *La Notte de San Lorenzo*—at least the part about the shooting stars. Between July 25 and August 18, the constellation Perseus becomes visible. It's considered the finest of all meteor showers. Especially after midnight, you can see as many as a hundred meteor showers an hour.

A.R. went into packing mode. Pilot to control tower, she thought. We're ready for take-off. I'm going to New York! La is coming to Kindbrae! And, to top it off, I have a birthday on August 20! I'll be ten years old.

A.R.'s thoughts of Space Cadet Camp seemed to drift far away. Right now, she was flying in her own personal galaxy.

Pappy came into A.R.'s bedroom, where she was busy packing. Around her lay piles of folded and unfolded T-shirts, shorts, jeans (clean and unclean), two backpacks, piles of CDs, towels, assorted jar lids of various sizes, thread spools, pens, string, rubber bands, a bicycle pump, and plastic soft-drink bottles (parts of an unfinished project to demonstrate rocket power).

"Here," he said, handing his daughter a canning jar filled with dirt.

"Dirt?" asked A.R. "My room is messy enough. I don't think I need dirt."

"I thought you might get homesick, so I'm sending along a little Minnesota soil to keep you company. Go ahead, open it," he coaxed.

"I bet Big Brother Billy put worms in here. I don't need worms. I'm not going fishing in New York," A.R. said as she followed her father's directions and emptied the jar of dirt on her desk. There were no worms, only what looked like a crumpled dollar bill.

But it wasn't a crumpled dollar bill.

"A hundred dollars!" A.R.'s eyes lit up like the mask in Dr. Troxler's truck.

"You hit pay dirt," Pappy said with a smile. "I think a trip to New York is one of those tremendously gigantic emergencies I've talked about. You earned it. You've been very responsible this summer."

"Pappy!" A.R. said as she hugged her father, leaving dirt prints on his clean white T-shirt as a souvenir.

Responsible, she thought. That's a nice sounding word.

Five A.M. A.R. watched the alarm clock and counted down. Three . . . two . . . one . . . *brring!* The estimated time of departure to the airport in Minneapolis–St. Paul was 5:45. She was right on schedule.

Mom had Flo Meisterteister look after the post office so she could take A.R. to the airport, accompany her through security, and present identification to the flight attendant.

Unlike the mornings when A.R. rode to the farmer's market, she did not nap in the car.

"Minn-plis, Sit Paul, 50 miles," A.R. announced

as she saw the familiar highway sign come into view.

If not for her seatbelt, A.R. would have been perched on the edge of her seat. She began to count and categorize things to pass the time: red cars, vans, yellow signs, green signs. When A.R. started to count low-flying airplanes, she knew the airport was near.

To help make the trip go faster, A.R. began to outline the remainder of the trip in her head: 12 more miles, park the car, check the luggage, go through the x-ray machine. Take off! A.R. ticked off each step as it happened. By the time she got through security, she didn't care. She was almost there.

"I'm Linda, your personal flight attendant for the trip. Anything you need, just ask me," said a young woman at the departure gate. Airline policy made sure that a child flying without an accompanying adult had an assigned flight attendant. A.R. not only had a personal flight attendant, she also had just met the woman who would become her new best friend all the way to New York.

"Some juice, Ms. Smith?" Linda asked.

"Cold cereal or a bagel, Ms. Smith? Would you like to read this magazine?"

Nothing, however, compared to the first question

she had asked A.R. "Would you like to visit the flight deck?"

Would she? After A.R. hugged her mother good-bye, Linda personally escorted her down the departure ramp, directly to the flight deck.

"Welcome aboard. So this is your first solo flight?" Captain Cunningham asked A.R. He showed her the control levers, the light instruments, and the flight engineer's panel. He even let A.R. sit in the captain's seat.

Later, as she fastened her seatbelt, A.R. thought to herself, my first solo flight. A.R. *did* feel responsible.

The time seemed to fly by. A.R. imagined each city below—Chicago, Detroit, Cleveland, Buffalo. She imagined people in each city were waving to her as she completed her first solo flight.

Before she knew it, the captain announced, "If you look over to the right side of the plane, you'll see we have a clear view of the Statue of Liberty." Her thoughts felt as light as air pockets. And like a plane in rough weather, her heart bucked.

Linda heard all about La from A.R., so she wasn't surprised when she saw La at the gate.

La was waiting at the arrival gate, dressed in black

and orange almost from head to toe—black socks and skirt; orange flowered blouse and orange sneakers and sunglasses. On her head was a big black hat with a floppy brim. It made her look like a jolly jack-o-lantern, A.R. thought as she ran toward her.

Linda went through the formalities of uniting her passenger with her grandmother. La took it from there.

"Did you pack for a month?" La asked as she lifted A.R.'s suitcase off the baggage carousel. Then they ran out to grab a taxi. Next stop: Brooklyn, New York.

The part of New York City where La lived reminded A.R. of a television program. Row after row of brownstones built over a century and a half ago stood like soldiers, one next to another in a slope all the way up the block to Prospect Park.

La's apartment was only a short refueling stop.

"Today we'll stay close to home," La announced, finishing her sentence after they were out the door.

They started with lunch at the Brooklyn Botanical Garden.

For the first afternoon of their tour, it seemed like La packed some of her memories in her purse. "I should've known that your pappy would become a farmer," La remarked as they passed the children's garden. "He spent every day here during the summer from the first day of vacation until the fall harvest."

"I should have known that your pappy would become a farmer." La remarked again as they walked through the Wildlife Center in Prospect Park. "He volunteered here as a teenager. He fed the seals and cleaned the cages. About the only thing he didn't do was dance with the wolves—and he would've done that if they let him."

La showed A.R. her secret paths through the park that led under antique tunnels and carved bridges, along streams, and to a waterfall that ended at Prospect Lake, where they fed the ducks. "I should have known that when your mom inherited the family farm, your pappy would take the challenge and become a farmer. I should have known that he wasn't going to become a musician.

"See, we have the country right here in the middle of the city," La was fond of reminding anyone who walked with her through the park.

"Well, come on. We've got a universe to explore," La frequently reminded her granddaughter.

At the New York Hall of Science, they danced, jumped, and ran through the Light and Sound exhibit while their shadows triggered music as they moved. As they stood on each side of the outdoor Science Playground, La talked softly in the Whisper Dish, while A.R. listened to her whispered message. The tiniest whisper was magnified when spoken into the dish.

Then they traded places. A.R. whispered into the dish as La had just done. Then, forgetting where she was, A.R. roared, "AFTER WE'RE DONE HERE, I HAVE TO GO TO THE BATHROOM."

"Oops," A.R. said, blushing and realizing that what she said into the Whisper Dish had sounded like it was broadcast over a loudspeaker.

"When was the last time you dined on an aircraft carrier?" La asked, as they were finishing up lunch at the Intrepid Sea and Air Space Museum. On this restored 900-foot-long aircraft carrier, they took a tour of a strategic missile submarine. Both A.R. and her grandmother waited patiently in the long line so they could fly a jet mission in the Navy flight simulator.

A.R. didn't answer. La thought she might be tired.

"A penny for your thoughts?" La asked.

That question sounds familiar, A.R. thought.

For the first time in days, thoughts about Space Cadet Camp were beginning to orbit. Then A.R. launched into telling her grandmother all about how she missed her chance to join. She began by describing her meeting with Becky Lambordini at the farmer's market, explained her grouchy night, and ended her story by repeating what she had said as she sat in the family room, "Life is just not fair."

"Maybe it's not too late for the camp's next session. Come on, let's get out of here," La said forcefully. "No time like the present. Let's go home. We'll check the Internet."

"The Internet. Duh . . . why didn't *I* think of that?" said A.R.

They rode the subway back to Brooklyn. Climbing out from under the streets of New York, grandmother and granddaughter acted more like sisters the way they laughed and had fun together. But they were on their way home with a serious purpose in mind.

La got online. The downloading began in earnest.

Key word: Exploration Channel

Search: Index

Select: Space Cadet Camp

Print: Application

Five pages came out of the printer, to be returned to the Exploration Channel in triplicate.

"*Triplicate* means we have to make three copies," La explained to A.R., who by this time was a little overwhelmed with everything she had to do.

"Roll up your sleeves and get to work," La directed.

"But this says I have to have a physical,"

A.R. complained as she read the form.

"My doctor is right down the street," La responded.

"I have to send them a copy of my grades, too," A.R. said.

"I'll call your mother right now and she can fax them to me," said La.

"I've got to write an essay: 'What do you think is the most exciting thing about visiting space?' I can't write!" A.R. grumbled.

"Of course you can. Here's paper. Here's a pen. Or write on the computer," La said, matter-of-factly.

A.R. couldn't seem to get started. She went to the kitchen and got a drink of water. She washed her hands for a long time, ate some crackers, and then returned to the computer. The computer clock in the lower right-hand corner showed that exactly 14 minutes had passed and nothing had been written. A.R. was perplexed.

Her grandmother had to think of something to get A.R. up and running. "Let's talk about it. Imagine you were living and working in outer space. What would be the most exciting part of it?" La coaxed.

"It's *all* exciting," A.R. responded. "I could see shooting stars up close. I'd go on moonwalks. I'd taste space food . . ." A.R.'s list went on.

"Yes, but the *most* exciting thing?" La asked.

"Well, this may sound stupid, but I've always wanted to be weightless." Then the words started to tumble out of her mouth. "Imagine how much fun it would be to juggle in outer space or turn somersaults. I'd love to find out how you wash your face. If there's no gravity, water could drift off in little bubbles all through the cabin. I wonder how you make a peanut-butter sandwich. You could scoop out the peanut butter and then flip it across the room and it would float right onto your bread. I bet in space you'd feel just like you do in a flying dream."

A.R. went on. She didn't see that La had a tape recorder going. After A.R. finished, La said to her, "Here, I got everything down on tape. Listen to it. We'll type it up on the computer, do a little editing, and your essay's done."

For La, every problem had a solution. That's what A.R. loved about her grandmother.

They mailed the essay out late that afternoon.

"Just wait until tomorrow," La reminded A.R. "We've got the best saved till last."

Like almost everything she did, La had a strategy

for their tour of the American Museum of Natural History. It is, after all, the largest natural history museum in the world. La knew exactly what they would do from the time they stepped into the Theodore Roosevelt Rotunda to the time they left. She wasn't about to waste time roaming aimlessly through the 42 halls of this museum.

La and A.R. began in a very down-to-earth way. They walked in the footsteps of dinosaurs. They explored the rain forests of Central Africa. They learned about giant squid and the wickedest sharks that lurked beneath the sea. But as the day went on, La couldn't stay earthbound, particularly when she had to show off the Rose Center for Earth and Space.

"Where, thanks to modern science, you can now see a starry sky from Manhattan!" La announced in an elaborate voice that sounded as if she were a paid advertisement for the Rose Center.

La had reason to be expressive. The Space Theater at the Rose Center is the largest virtual reality simulator in the world. "I can't believe it myself," she said, "and this is my nineteenth visit here since it opened a year ago. This is where cutting-edge technology is razor sharp," La went on. "Trust me, you're about to soar through our galaxy. And, best of all—the theater was named after you. But they ran out of money just when they were going to spell out A-i-d-a," La pointed out as they purchased tickets for the show.

"We have exactly one hour until show time at the Space Theater," A.R. reminded La.

"Perfect!" La said. "Let's go shopping."

They went into the museum gift shop. A.R. still had some of the pay dirt that Pappy gave her before she left. The museum shop was the perfect place to buy souvenirs for her family and friends in Minnesota. And La had her own shopping to do.

As they were paying for their purchases, La asked, "How about two soda pops before blastoff?"

"OK, Captain," A.R. responded.

From the museum gift shop they headed to the museum's cafeteria.

"I've got an idea!" La exclaimed after they sat down. And when La was struck with an idea, she lit up. It seemed to A.R. like a lightbulb popped up over her head, just like in the cartoons.

"Close your eyes," La insisted.

"La . . . " A.R.'s voice trailed off suspiciously.

"Come on," La continued. "I promise you'll like this."

"OK," A.R. said and scrunched her eyes shut.

Something went "squish" on the tip of her nose. "Ugh!" A.R. said, feeling a cool blob of goo right on the tip of her nose.

"La!" she hollered.

"What?" La said as she quickly pulled a mirror out of her purse and placed it in front of A.R. "See? Nothing. But don't touch your nose!" La then pulled out a jar of Major Owens' Glow-in-the-Dark Goop and Paint.

"Just think of what you'll look like tonight after dark," La said. And then she handed the goop and brush to A.R. "It's your turn."

La and A.R. giggled and giggled as they painted. The other customers in the cafeteria stared at the two of them, but A.R. and La went right on creating their face art.

They were still giggling as they relaxed into their seats in the Space Theater. As the lights began to dim, A.R. and La began to glow.

"Look!" yelled a boy in the audience as he pointed to where A.R. and La were seated. Soon twitters of laughter began to mix with the sound system. For a few minutes, the show overhead was dimmed by the show in the audience.

There sat A.R. and La, lit up like the cosmos. Thanks to Major Owens' Glow-in-the-Dark

Goop and Paint—and not modern technology—there were two shows for the price of one that day at the Space Theater.

That night, when grandmother and grand-daughter went outside on the back deck of her apartment, they still glowed. "Should I sell tickets to the Aida Rose Space Theater?" La asked. Their giggles lit up the night like fireflies blinking on and off in the darkening air.

And then they packed their bags for the flight back to Kindbrae.

CHAPTER 7

Ten, Nine, Eight, Seven, Six . . . BLASTOFF!

The people in Kindbrae called August "the dog days" for their own reasons. The usually frisky Troxund was a perfect example of how August got its nickname around Kindbrae. He'd dig a cool, dark hole in shaded ground and lie there most of the day.

When the August heat in New York seemed to bake the city and the air was as thick as pea soup, La closed up shop.

"I design and sell gloves. My customers are brides, rock stars, and construction workers. I make the prettiest, toughest, and warmest gloves money can buy. But who needs gloves in August?" La would explain.

So she'd pack up her telescope, observation charts, and her maps for stargazing and visit Kindbrae.

"Kindbrae," she would remind A.R., "is where the

nights are clear and dark. No city lights to block the wonders of the skies."

Since A.R. and La arrived in Kindbrae only hours before the Night of the Shooting Stars, there was little time to waste. Usually La arrived a few days early. She liked to have her portable star lab set up. And she liked time to build enthusiasm and tell family stories about who saw a shooting star and whose dreams had come true.

But this summer, La didn't have that kind of time. Moments after she arrived in Kindbrae, La chose a spot in the fields not too far from the house to await the darkening sky.

Seems like La must have also unpacked perfect weather. Although there had been a rainy spell, the sky on *La Notte de San Lorenzo* danced with stars. Mom, Pappy, and Big Brother Billy joined her and A.R. The family treated this night like a holiday—their very own New Year's Eve when everyone could stay up until midnight. Each person hoped to see a shooting star. And who wouldn't want his or her dreams to come true?

La was full of facts and challenges that night: "Imagine, we can see more than 3,000 separate stars. Should we count them?"

"Quick! Point to the northern star."

"Ah, the Milky Way. The heart of our galaxy. Think about it—over 100 billion stars!"

Everyone took turns looking through the telescope while the others had their eyes glued to the sky in hopes of seeing a shooting star. What didn't explode in the heavens, A.R. made up for on Earth. She was bursting with stories about her adventures with La in New York.

The timed passed quickly.

"It's ten to twelve," Mom announced.

The children moaned with disappointment, but both A.R. and Big Brother Billy were secretly glad the night was coming to an end even though they didn't see a shooting star. They could barely keep their eyes open. An hour earlier, Pappy had found a nice soft spot in the grass and went to sleep.

"Sort of looks like Troxund these days, doesn't he?" Mom laughed as she pointed to her husband.

La stayed out for another hour.

The next morning A.R. remembered that she had a flying dream. She and La were picking flowers in the sky. Except that each flower was a star. A.R. liked that.

La's visits were a welcome change in the Smith household. Dinners became splashy celebrations. The table was set with candles and fresh flowers. And La delighted in cooking. She had fancy recipes for fresh summer vegetables and herbs picked from the garden. She made salad with fresh peas, radishes, roasted succotash with sweet corn, and lentils. Family and friends begged her to make her cherry pie. Pappy and Mom sure liked not having to think about what to put on the table for supper.

Flo and Lloyd once offered La a job as chef at the Kindbrae General Store and Cafe, but she turned them down. She was not one to make hamburgers and frog legs.

Each night after supper, A.R. would join her grandmother wherever La had set up her telescope. Each night they made time to wish upon a star. And for those first nights, A.R. had only one wish: "I wish I may, I wish I might get into Space Cadet Camp tonight."

Some days Big Brother Billy would go rowing with La on Kindbrae Lake. Or he'd try to exhaust her on long bicycle rides.

"I need my exercise," La insisted. "I keep in shape at my Brooklyn gym. I'm not about to go to seed here in the country."

Kindbrae noticed the change when La was in town. A.R. didn't make her daily visits to the Kindbrae

General Store and Cafe. But sometimes grandmother and granddaughter would ride their bikes into town to meet Mrs. Smith at the post office at closing time.

On one of those visits, Mom handed an envelope to A.R. with a return address that read, *The Exploration Channel, Space Cadet Camp.*

"It's here! It's here!" A.R. hooted and hollered when her mother gave her the letter.

"You're gonna wake up the chickens with all that noise," Mom said.

"Maybe she can try out for the town emergency warning siren," La remarked.

A.R. wasn't listening. She was reading the letter.

Dear Aida Rose Smith,

Thank you for your interest in Space Cadet Camp. We read your essay with interest, but we are sorry to inform you that your application reached us after the closing deadline.

We hope that you will apply next year. Remember our motto: The sky's the limit!

Sincerely yours,

Otis Starre

Admissions

"Well, this letter's short, but not too sweet," La commented as she read the letter.

Mrs. Smith hugged her daughter.

There was quiet all around. This was one of those times when saying nothing meant saying everything.

When they got home, A.R. quietly went to her room. She tinkered for awhile with an old sundial she had made from a flowerpot and a stick. She flicked her flashlight on and off at the glow-in-the-dark solar system that was pasted overhead. Then she buried her head in her pillow.

Her mother came up to look in on her. "La and I will take care of your afternoon chores."

"OK," said A.R., and they left it at that.

A.R. came down to the kitchen a little before dinnertime. Mom and La were deep in conversation.

"How are you doing?" La asked.

"OK," A.R. replied.

"I think tonight calls for one of your favorite suppers—pasta with fresh basil and those heavenly tomatoes from your garden," said La.

"OK," A.R. replied again.

"Your mom and I have some talking we have to finish up. Grown-up stuff. Can you give us a little time to finish our chat?" La asked.

"OK," A.R. said, and got on her bicycle and rode to her secret place down by the Kindbrae Dump and Recycling Center. She thought about the games she played with Becky Lambordini. Why didn't Becky write? Then she thought about her friend Lily Sue, who was away on vacation. She walked by a discarded can that didn't make it to the recycling bin. She kicked it.

I guess it's OK, she thought. It's all OK. A-OK, over and out.

The next morning A.R. was surprised to see La up so early. She was wearing pink-and-white-striped overalls and a wide-brimmed straw hat covered with silk flowers.

"The gardening gloves are my original design," she pointed out. They were pink with little blue bows sewn around each cuff. "Do I look like a farmer?" she asked her son.

"You couldn't if you tried," he answered.

And to A.R. she said, "Ms. Lacracia, your new farmhand, reporting for work."

La tried hard to make jokes, tell stories, and make up riddles to cheer up her granddaughter.

Toward midmorning, A.R. turned to La and said, "Grandma, you make me happy just the way things are. I just don't want to laugh today. OK?"

"OK," said La. And then she thought, 'Grandma'—maybe I like the sound of that word.

A.R. went back to staking the tomatoes. She was going to be ten years old in a few days and she had responsibilities.

More just-OK days followed, but the star-filled nights still remained special. A.R. counted the days until her birthday. And each night she joined La, who never tired of pointing out the August stars.

A.R. thought that this summer Mom, Pappy, and La were having more than the usual grown-ups-only conversations. And they seemed to increase the closer it got to her birthday. She noticed, too, that there were more hushed telephone conversations.

Too many family meetings, A.R. thought. Grown-ups have too many worries.

Little mention was made of A.R.'s tenth birthday until the morning itself, when Mrs. Smith shared the plans with her daughter.

"Tonight the whole family's going out for a nice birthday dinner at the Cafe," Mom announced.

You've got to be kidding, A.R. thought to herself, but didn't say anything. It's frog legs night! That's *not* OK.

With the added daylight of summer, Pappy usually worked later in the fields, but not on birthday night. The family was cleaned up and ready to go into town by 5:30 P.M.—all except Big Brother Billy, who had made plans with his friend Dillon.

"Let's go in the back entrance," Pappy said as he pulled the car in right behind the back door that led to the storeroom and kitchen. This was kind of different, A.R. thought. Flo didn't like people walking through the kitchen, but she didn't say anything as the family edged around her and her pots and pans.

"SURPRISE!" everyone yelled as the Smiths appeared in the store.

The ceiling glowed with twinkle lights. Flo had also crocheted and hung dozens of stars that she had starched so they'd hold their shape. A table was filled with food and presents.

A.R. looked around, her eyes as big as saucers. Lily Sue and her family were there. A.R. was even more surprised to see that Thien Van Nhu, his sister Le Mai, and Mr. and Mrs. Van Nhu drove nearly a hundred miles from their farm. And Milo and his family drove almost as far.

No one expected that the Kindbrae townsfolk would stay home. Dr. Troxler, Delphinium and Mel Beck, Roberta and Bob Bobbe—all were there. The Bobbes had Shawn hooked up to their wagon outside so that the kids could have hayrides. Trixie O'Rourke brought the twins. Tiny Sybrandt came with Big Glenn. They brought along a few things from the Kindbrae Dump and Recycling Center for party favors (discarded books, soap bottles made into hanging planters, coasters made from roof tiles— things like that).

Big Brother Billy and Dillon arrived all wrapped up in bubble wrap, which they had bound around themselves with duct tape. They were wearing their football helmets. They were supposed to be astronauts. They presented A.R. with a backpack that Flo had embroidered with A.R.'s initials, stars, and rocket ships. (Flo was as good at the art of embroidery as she was at crocheting.)

About a half-hour into the party, there was a commotion at the door.

"I'm sorry we're late," someone said. A.R. recognized the voice. There were Becky Lambordini and her family. Her parents began shaking hands and hugging their old friends.

La smiled, pleased with herself that all the hushed plans she had made and all the telephone calls had worked out.

"Here," Becky said as she handed a present to A.R. Then Becky began her story, hardly taking a breath. "I went to the head of the camp and I told him all about you and us and he knew that I was talking about you because he said that he had just received an application from you and that it was postmarked too late. And I even told him about your sign at the farmer's market that everyone at camp thought was so clever with the cabbages that looked like Saturn and the rocket ship carrots. And so I asked him, well here—open it." Becky finally came up for air.

"A Space Cadet shirt!" A.R. beamed.

"Look at the name tag," Becky insisted. "And read the letter!"

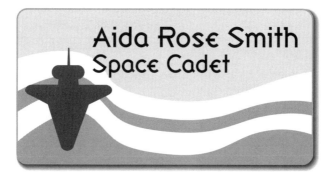

Dear Miss Smith,

Your interest in space exploration, as told to us by Miss Lambordini, has earned you the award of Honorary Space Cadet. We look forward to having you join us next summer in our Space Cadet Program. Get ready for blastoff!

Sincerely yours

Otto Orbit

Otto Orbit
Founder and Captain

That night, everyone stood outside the Kindbrae General Store and Cafe, hugging and kissing good-bye. A.R. looked overhead. A shooting star zoomed through the sky.

And as it did, it seemed as if the mask in Dr. Troxler's truck winked back at it.

Becky's family stayed overnight at the Smith's house, so La asked Becky and A.R. to walk home from the cafe with her.

"For one last look at the stars over Kindbrae," La said, pleased that she had someone new to tell all about *La Notte de San Lorenzo*. "Tomorrow I'll be back in New York."

"I'm going to share a little secret," La said in a hushed voice. "After everyone went to bed on the Night of the Shooting Stars, I stayed up another hour or so. It was 1:03 A.M. I charted the time. It was then that I *did* see a shooting star." And then she paused. "Do you think a grandmother can pass on her dreams to her granddaughter?"

There was a thoughtful silence.

La's question seemed to put a close on the summer.

Before she left, La guaranteed everyone that she'd be back to watch the Milky Way next summer. A.R. was already looking forward to her new responsibilities as a ten-year-old, to Space Camp, and, of course, to seeing La again.

At the airport, La hugged her granddaughter heart to heart. She said with a knowing smile, "OK, Ms. Smith, you're ready to blast off."

"OK!" A.R. answered emphatically. "OK, over and out."